P9-CEK-366

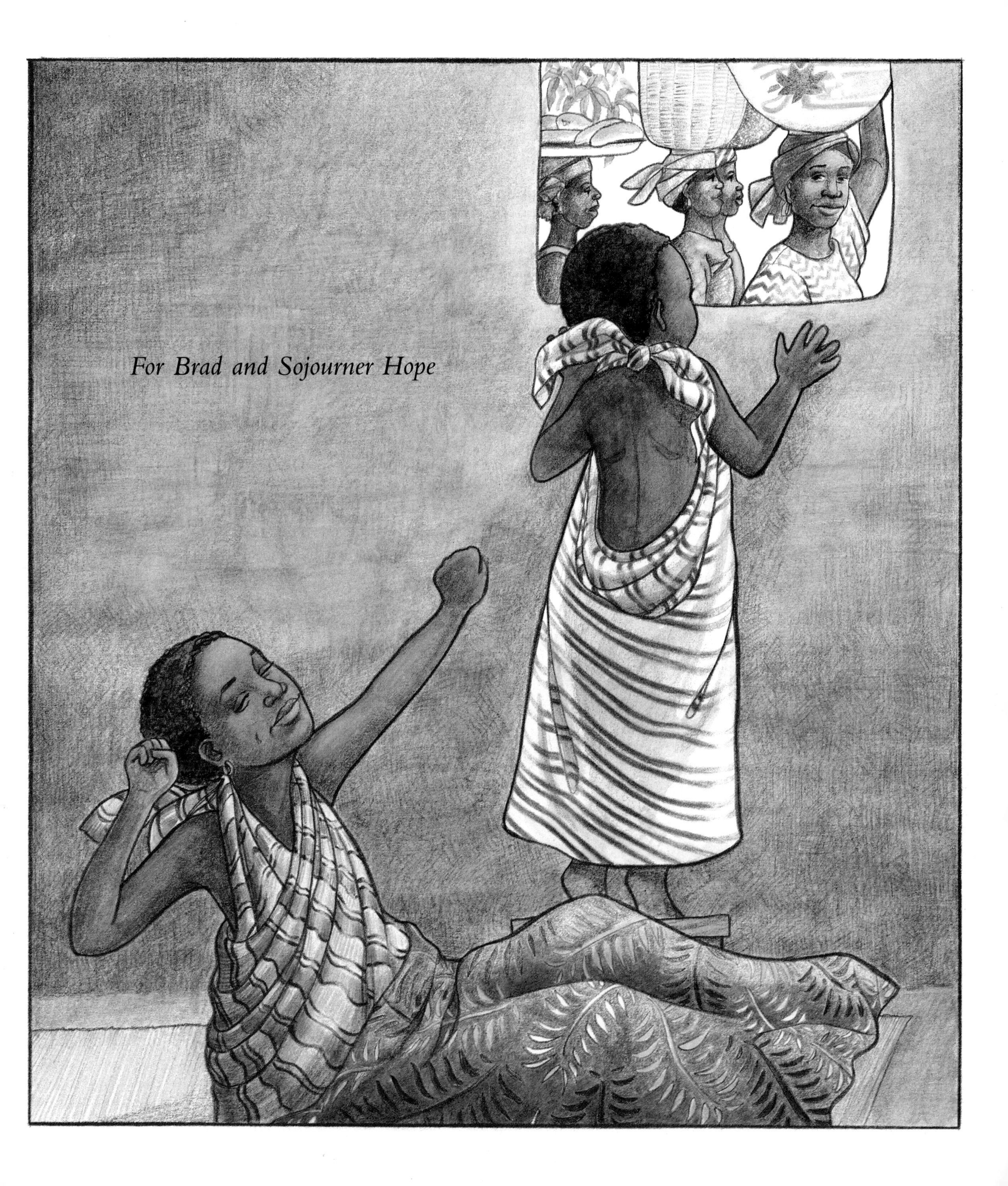

For Brad and Sojourner Hope

 Published by Scholastic Press, a division of Scholastic Inc.,
Publishers since 1920.

Library of Congress Cataloging-in-Publication Data
Cowen-Fletcher, Jane.
It takes a village / written and illustrated by Jane Cowen-Fletcher,
p. cm.
Summary: On market day in a small village in Benin, Yemi tries to watch her little brother Kokou and finds out that the entire village is watching out for him, too.

ISBN 0-590-46573-2

[1. Benin–Fiction. 2. Brothers and sisters–Fiction.]
I. Title.
PZ7.C8358It 1993
[E]–dc20 CIP
AC

24 23 22 21 20 19 18 17 16 15 14 13
Printed in the U.S.A.
First edition, January 1994

Book Design by Adrienne Syphrett
The illustrations in this book were done in colored pencil with watercolor washes.

Pronunciation of Names

Kokou (KOH · koo)
Yemi (YEH · me)

Thanks to Bruce McMillan for his guidance and enthusiasm; to Florence Ogah Bellini, Hanna Bulger, Steve Connors, Joan O'Brien, and Cathy Scala for reference help and support; to the Peace Corps for the opportunity to live and work in Benin; and very special thanks to the people of Benin, especially to the residents of Sé who were such gracious neighbors for two years, and who taught me by their example the profound importance of community.

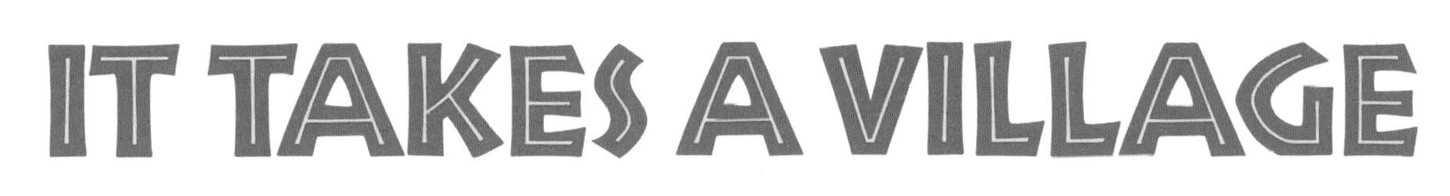

IT TAKES A VILLAGE

Written and illustrated by Jane Cowen-Fletcher

SCHOLASTIC PRESS • NEW YORK

The sun was just beginning to climb into the sky. But the villagers had been up for hours. It was market day.

"Yemi," Mama said, "you must take care of your little brother today while we're at the market. I will be too busy selling our mangoes."

"Come, Kokou," Yemi said, "I will watch you today, all by myself!"

"All by yourself?" Mama asked, and smiled at what Yemi said. Mama knew better.

Mama picked up their mangoes. Yemi picked up Kokou. She felt very grown-up as she walked out of the family compound beside Mama.

They joined the stream of people walking into the village. People came from all around to sell their goods and buy whatever they needed. Market day was also a time for visiting.

The greetings started the moment they stepped on the paths into town.

"Hello!"

"How are you?"

"How is your family?"

Yemi helped Mama set out their mangoes. One of the other fruit vendors said, "Yemi is a big girl now. She is a lot of help to you!"

"Yes," said Mama, "she is going to watch Kokou for me today."

"All by myself," Yemi added.

"All by yourself? *Yay gay*!" the women marveled. They smiled and nodded, but they knew better, too.

When the mangoes were all in neat piles, Yemi asked if she and Kokou could take a look around the market. Mama said, "Yes, but don't be gone too long."

Yemi had not walked very far when Kokou became restless. “He must be hungry,” she said. She set him down for just one minute so she could buy some peanuts. . .

. . .and Kokou wandered off.

"*Cho*!" Yemi cried when she turned around and discovered Kokou was gone. She put the peanuts in her pocket...

...and she hurried off to find him.

"Where could he have gone?" she said.
As Yemi searched for him, she began to worry.
"Kokou must be hungry."

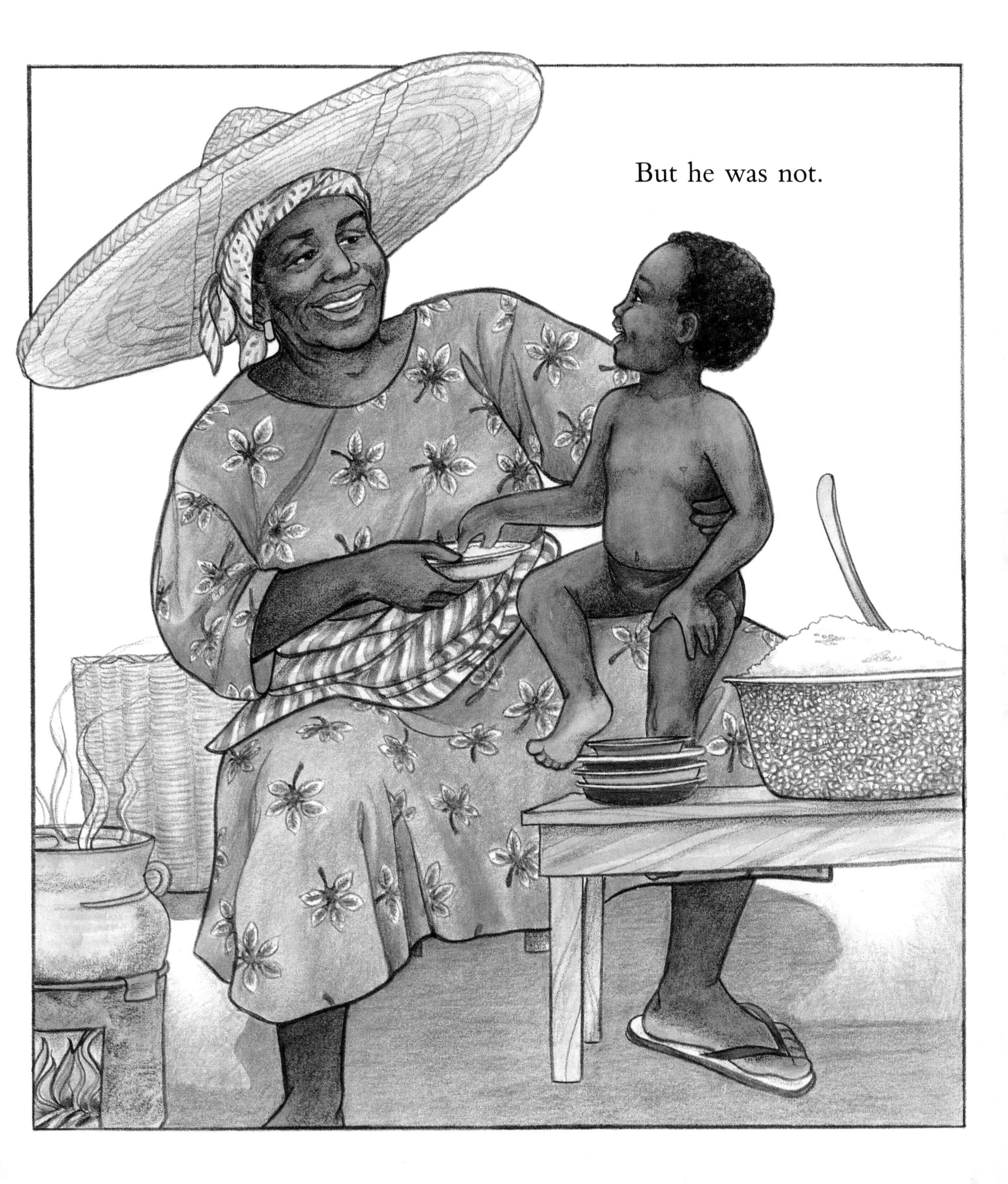

But he was not.

“Kokou must be thirsty.”

But he was not.

"Kokou must be frightened."

But he was not.

"Kokou must be hot."

But he was not.

“Kokou must be tired.”

But he was not.

Finally, after searching for him everywhere,
Yemi stopped and cried aloud, "Kokou must be lost!"

But he was not.

Just across the path from where Yemi stood, Kokou was waking up.

"Is this your Kokou?" the mat vendor asked.

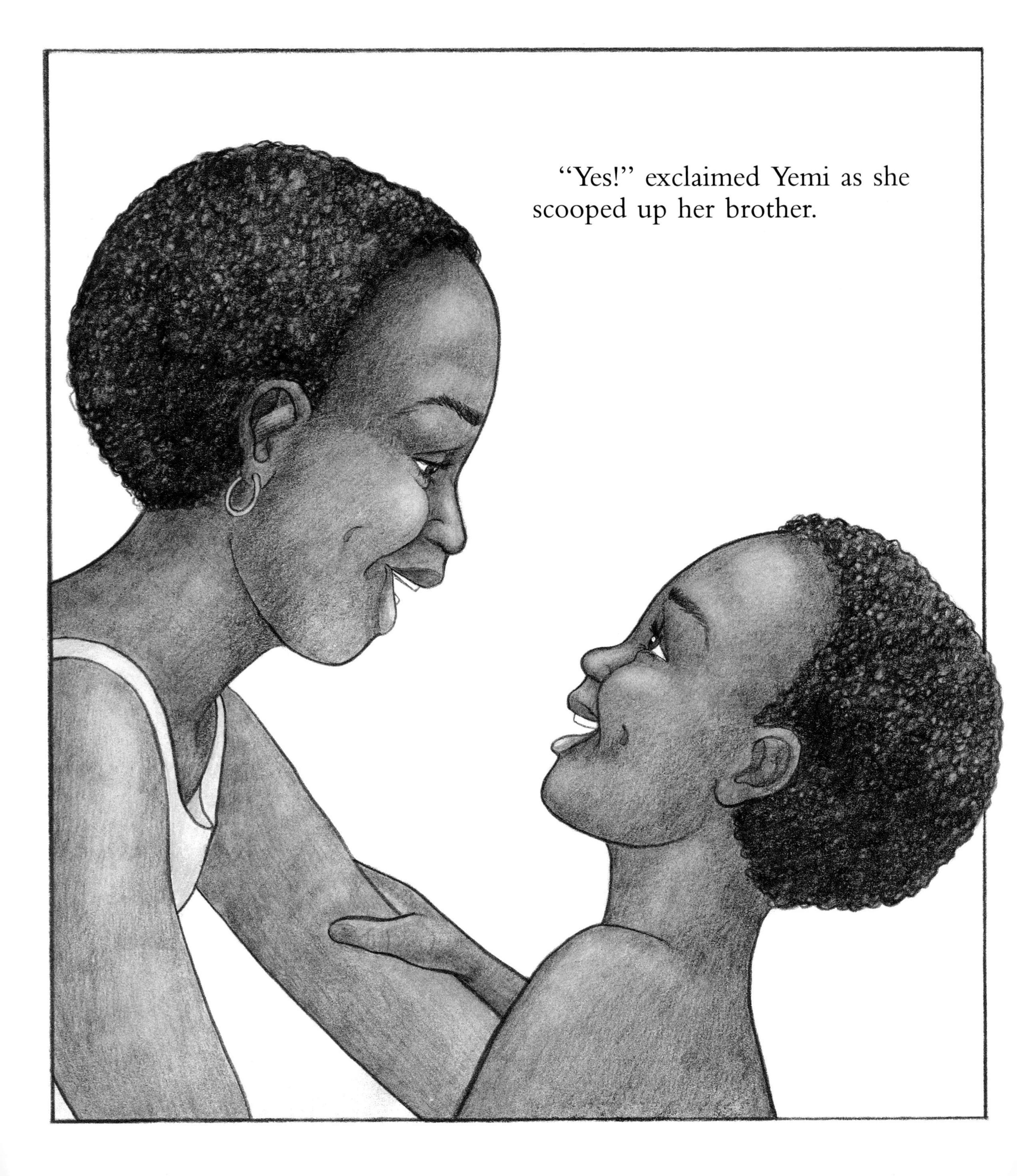

"Yes!" exclaimed Yemi as she scooped up her brother.

"Thank you so much for taking care of him," Yemi said to the mat vendor.

"Oh," he chuckled, "I was not the only one." He pointed to where Kokou had come from.

Yemi thanked him again and headed off in that direction.

She said, "Thank you," again. . .

and again. . .

and again. . .

and again.

"We've been gone a long time, Kokou," Yemi said. "Mama must be worried."

But she was not. Mama knew better. "As my mama told me, and her mama told her, I will tell you. You weren't alone today, Yemi. We don't raise our children by ourselves. 'It takes a village to raise a child.'"

The Market

Africa has its share of supermarkets and shopping centers, but in rural villages in Benin, and many other African countries, the traditional open-air market is the only market that serves the community, as it has for hundreds of years. The villagers are the buyers and sellers. Market days occur on a regular schedule the year round. The produce and other food staples available vary according to growing season and region.

The market is also the source for fabric, clothes, cooking utensils, farm tools, fishing equipment, livestock, hand-crafted items like baskets and pottery, as well as such imported items as canned milk, canned fish, batteries, lanterns, soaps, plastic dishes, enamel pots, pens, and school notebooks. It's an open-air shopping mall where you're likely to find just about anything.

Market day is also a social occasion with food vendors selling hot meals, snacks, and beverages. It's an opportunity to visit with relatives and friends.

All of the items depicted in this book — such as the pottery, fabrics, baskets, decorated calabashes, and so on — though not representative of a specific region, are typically found in markets throughout Benin.

It takes a village to raise a child.

—African Proverb